Ju
F
Sh 6   Shiefman, Vicky.
         Sunday potatoes, Monday
potatoes.

Temple Israel Library
Minneapolis, Minn.
———

Please sign your full name on the above card.

Return books promptly to the Library or Temple Office.

Fines will be charged for overdue books or for damage or loss of same.

DEM60

SUNDAY POTATOES, MONDAY POTATOES

by Vicky Shiefman

illustrated by
Louise August

SIMON & SCHUSTER BOOKS FOR YOUNG READERS
Published by Simon & Schuster
New York   London   Toronto   Sydney   Tokyo   Singapore

Thank you, Chef Lorenzo Berman

SIMON & SCHUSTER BOOKS FOR YOUNG READERS
Simon & Schuster, Rockefeller Center, 1230 Avenue of the Americas, New York, New York 10020.
Text copyright © 1994 by Vicky Shiefman. Illustrations copyright © 1994 by Louise August. All rights
reserved including the right of reproduction in whole or in part in any form. SIMON & SCHUSTER BOOKS
FOR YOUNG READERS is a trademark of Simon & Schuster. Designed by Lucille Chomowicz. The text of
this book is set in Cloister Bold. The illustrations were done in linoleum cuts and paint. Manufactured in
the United States of America   10   9   8   7   6   5   4   3   2   1
Library of Congress Cataloging-in-Publication Data
Shiefman, Vicky.   Sunday potatoes, Monday potatoes   by Vicky Shiefman ; illustrated by Louise August.
p.   cm.   Summary: A poor family eats potatoes each day of the week except on Saturday when they
eat their special potato pudding. Recipe is included.   [1. Potatoes—Fiction.]   I. August, Louise, ill.
II. Title.   PZ7.S5547Su   1994   [E]—dc20   92–46112 √ CIP   ISBN 0-671-86596-X

To my mother, Emma

VS

To Mom, Tanta, Peter, Margalit, Alon,
Danny, Rani, and Roy — with love

LA

At one time there was a country.

In that country there was a town.

In that town there was a street.

In that street
there was a house.

In that house there was a room.
In that room sat a family.
They were very poor.
All they had to eat
was potatoes.
You may ask,
did they like to eat potatoes

Well,
they did like to eat!

So, they cut potatoes.

Planted,

and dug
potatoes.

grew,

Stored,

washed,

and cooked potatoes.

On Sunday they ate potatoes.

Monday, they ate potatoes.

Tuesday, potatoes.

Wednesday, potatoes.

Thursday, potatoes.

Friday, potatoes.

But, on Saturday,
guess what they ate.

Potato pudding!

And they ate
and ate

and ate

and ate

until it was all gone.

Saturday: POTATO PUDDING

serves 6

Ingredients

5-6 large potatoes, peeled

1 cup butter

½ cup flour

1 cup milk

½ cup grated cheese
   (cheddar, swiss, or provolone)

2 yellow onions

1 teaspoon thyme

1 teaspoon salt (optional)

1 teaspoon pepper

1. Boil potatoes. Cool.

2. Grate potatoes finely.

3. Drain grated potatoes on paper towel.

4. Melt butter.

5. In large bowl, combine butter and flour. Stir until smooth.

6. Add milk and grated cheese.

7. Peel and chop onions. Cook in saucepan with 1-2 tablespoons butter for about 15 minutes or until golden brown.

8. Add onions to cheese mixture.

9. Add thyme, salt, and pepper.

10. Add grated potatoes. Stir until all ingredients are blended.

11. Spread mixture into greased 10″ x 7″ baking pan.

12. Bake about 40 minutes at 400° (until a brown crust forms).

13. Serve hot. Enjoy.

Temple Israel
Minneapolis, Minnesota

IN HONOR OF THE BAR MITZVAH OF

DAVID BERTIN GREENE

FROM HIS PARENTS,

KIM & CLIFF GREENE

October 14, 1995